Many Thanks,
"Quinn The Eskimo"
Gerald B. Mirra

MW00912006

The Fancy Shawl Dancer

by Gerald B. Mirra
Illustrated by Cindy Mayer-Strosser

Signature Publishing
P.O. Box 5599
Endicott, New York 13763-5599

The Fancy Shawl Dancer. © 1997 by Gerald B. Mirra. Printed and bound in the United States of America. All rights reserved. No part of this book may be reproduced in any form or by any electronic or mechanical means, including information storage and retrieval systems, without permission in writing from the publisher, except by a reviewer who may quote brief passages in a review. Published by Signature Books, Endicott, New York. First edition.

ISBN 0-9655486-1-9

This book is dedicated to
Andrea Reto
my partner in life and beyond

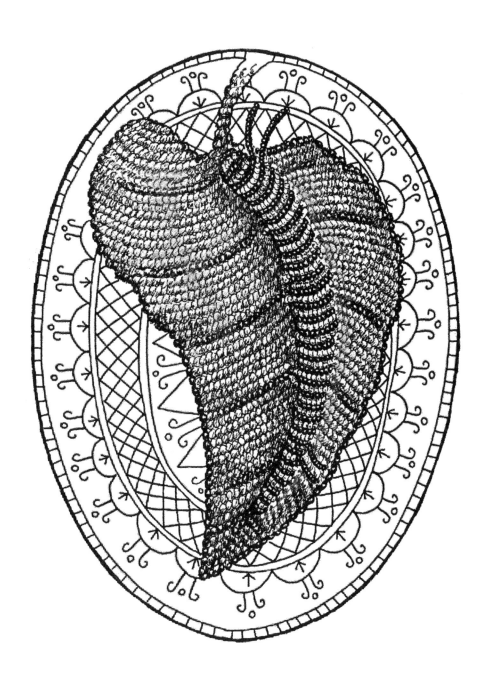

Chapter One

The school bus stopped at the Seneca Indian Reservation at 3:30 sharp. Sonja gathered her books and got off the bus.

The sun peeked through the clouds. The air smelled of sweet grass and meadow flowers. The clouds were big floating puff balls, drifting across the sky. It was a perfect day for dreamers.

Sonja walked a short distance through the woods and across the meadow to her home. She had done this for two years, every day after school.

Along her path she spotted a Monarch butterfly. It rested on top of a milkweed flower. She walked slowly toward the flower. She was careful not to frighten the butterfly.

Sonja watched the butterfly flap its wings. The Monarch danced across the center of the flower. It turned around, dancing gracefully. First it danced to the left. Then it danced to the right. Sonja could almost hear its wings flap.

Pitter-patter. Pitter-patter. Pitter-patter.

Sonja set her books on the ground. She spread her arms carefully. She began to dance around the flower gently. First she danced to the left. Then she danced to the right. She paused, and flapped her arms like the wings of the Monarch. It made her feel free.

The warm sun spread across her back.

Sonja slid her hand under the butterfly. It danced across her palm. She carefully put the butterfly in her lunch box. She would take very good care of it.

4

Sonja walked down the path to the front door of her home, singing. Her mother met her at the door.

"Well, you're sure happy today," said her mother.

"Mom, do you believe butterflies can dance?"

"That's a funny question," her mother said. "Why do you ask?"

"I was dancing with one today," said Sonja.

Her mother paused, waiting.

"Mom, do you believe in me?" asked Sonja.

"Always," said her mother. "Always and forever. But what is this about?"

Sonja took a deep breath. "I want to be a fancy shawl dancer. I want to perform at pow-wows."

"What about your school work? It would be hard to travel to pow-wows and go to school."

"I don't like school," said Sonja.

"But you have to go to school, dear."

"Mother, I want to dance. Will you let me?"

"Talk to your grandmother," her mother said. "She was a dancer long ago."

Sonja had great respect for her grandmother. Most Indian children do. She believed that the moon in the sky was grandmother. Her grandmother was full of wisdom.

Sonja sat down at the kitchen table and started her homework. She frowned at her books without even knowing she was doing it.

"I am not saying no," her mother reminded her. "But homework first. And then we have to make supper."

Sonja worked on her math. She looked over it carefully to make sure it was right. She didn't want to hurry and make mistakes.

8

When supper was finished, Sonja and her mother began to wash the dishes.

"Sonja, why do you want to be a pow-wow dancer?" asked her mother.

"When I dance, I am part of the earth," said Sonja. "I am part of the sky. I am important."

"Most young girls your age help the older women with their laundry," said her mother. "They help with the sewing and chores. Those are all important jobs."

"Mother, I want to *dance,*" said Sonja.

Her mother smiled. "When the dishes are done, then, go and talk to your grandmother. She taught me all I know. I will never be wiser than she is."

10

Sonja gathered her books and lunch box. She went outside. She opened her lunch box and put the butterfly in the palm of her hand. The butterfly danced to the warm spring air.

Sonja flapped her arms like the butterfly and danced. First to the left—then to the right. The butterfly disappeared.

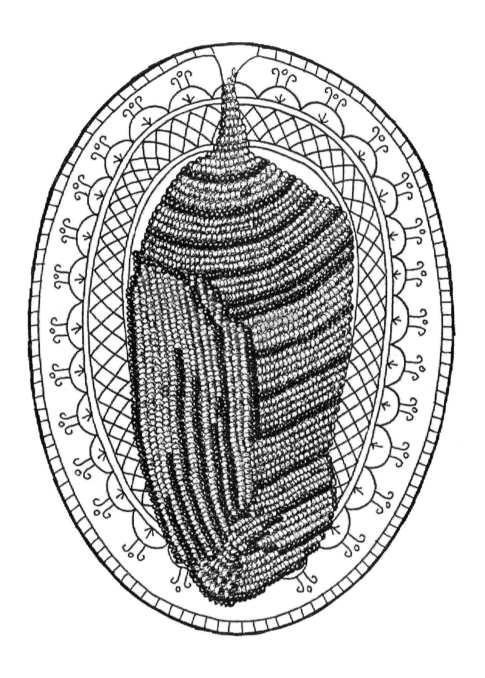

Chapter Two

The gentle breeze bent the shafts of field grass and meadow flowers.

Sonja walked through the field to her grandmother's door.

"Grandmother Ladyhawk, I come to talk to you about something very important," said Sonja.

Her grandmother let her in. "What is it you want to talk about, Sonja?"

"I want to be a fancy shawl dancer. I want to dance for people at pow-wows."

"Well, certainly you came to the right person," said Grandmother Ladyhawk with a smile.

"Grandmother, I don't want to go to school. I don't want to read and write. I just want to be a dancer."

"Child, I was once a dancer, too. I danced at Iroquois ceremonies and social dances. But I also learned to read and write."

14

Sonja did not argue. She respected her grandmother too much for that.

"I will make you a promise," said Grandmother Ladyhawk after a pause. "Help me with a bit of sewing. Then I will tell you an Indian legend about a fancy shawl dancer."

Grandmother went to another room. She came back with a pile of Indian trade cloth. She had bright fancy colors: blues, reds, yellows and whites. She had strands of fancy fringe and colored yarns.

Grandmother began cutting the cloth into different shapes and sizes. Sonja joined in and helped her.

"Sonja, there was once a great warrior among the Iroquois. He was a great leader of his people. He taught them, and loved them, but he was also respected outside the reservation. His wife was a great dancer. She had a beautiful outfit for dancing. She understood what many Indians could not because she could read and write books.

"This dancer wore red for respect. She respected her ancestors and their history. She was proud of where she came from. She wore blue for generosity. She tried to give kindness and understanding to her friends, her family, and strangers.

"This dancer wore yellow, the color of brotherhood. She loved all people, whether they were Indians or not. She wore white for wisdom.

"She wore all these colors in her dance outfit, and she danced very proud. And after her warrior became the sun in the sky, she still danced, in honor of him. She sees him every day, and she is never without him. She wrote a book about him."

"Who was this great warrior, Grandmother?"

"He was your grandfather, Sonja. Grandfather Soaring Eagle. And the dancer was me."

16

Sonja and her grandmother pinned and stitched the outfit together. The leggings were of blue cloth. The dress was yellow. The shawl was blue. The fringe was red, and hung all the way from the arms to the leggings.

Sonja asked, "What is it we are making, grandmother?"

"This is your shawl. I will teach you the dances that I know. You will have to learn the fancy shawl dance on your own. But when you go to the pow-wow, practice your dancing by the bench with the other dancers. Make sure you sit on the bench. Your chance will come."

"Thank you, grandmother!" said Sonja.

"Wait, child. You must agree to do something for me," said Grandmother. "You must study and work hard in school. Indian children must learn twice. They must learn of their people and learn of their history. They must also learn to live in the world outside of the reservation. This is why I am called Ladyhawk. I learned the dance of Soaring Eagle who lives among all people."

"Yes, grandmother," said Sonja gratefully. "I promise."

She hugged the bright colors against her body. She was going to be a dancer!

Chapter Three

The very next weekend Sonja and her mother travelled to the Wounded Knee Pow-wow. There were many Indian dancers from all over the country. Their outfits were bright and beautiful.

Sonja danced the opening ceremony, called the Grand Entry. Then the dance competition began. All of the dancers who would compete had numbers pinned to their outfits, and they sat together on the dancer's bench. There was no more room on the bench, so Sonja stood behind it, practicing her dance. The other dancers turned their heads and watched her.

One young Indian girl walked towards the dancers' bench. She tried to get the other dancers to move over. But they wouldn't let her sit down.

Sonja felt worried. "What if they don't let me sit down either?" she thought.

Sonja's hands began to sweat. Her grandmother had said she must sit on the dancers' bench. One of the older dancers moved, just a little, and now there was room for one more small dancer.

An older dancer by the open seat was reading a book. Sonja slipped onto the bench next to her.

"What are you reading?" asked Sonja.

"A book about a great warrior named Soaring Eagle," replied the older dancer.

"He is my grandfather," Sonja said.

"What is your name?"

"Sonja," she replied.

"I saw you dancing behind the bench. Do you want to be a dancer?"

"Oh, yes! More than anything in the whole world," said Sonja.

The dancer smiled. "I feel very tired. I don't know if I can dance today. Will you take my place?"

Sonja felt scared. Suddenly she didn't know if she could get up in front of everyone and dance. But Grandmother had said her chance would come—and here it was.

"Oh, yes, please!" said Sonja.

The girl took off the contest number that was pinned to her outfit. She gave it to Sonja. Then she walked to the judges and told them Sonja was to dance in her place.

When Sonja walked to the middle of the dance area she was shaking. She remembered her grandmother. She remembered her grandfather. And she remembered the butterfly. Sonja raised her arms. She turned to the left. She turned to the right. And at that very moment, a Monarch butterfly landed on her shoulder.

Pitter-patter. Pitter-patter. Pitter-patter.

Sonja reached for the sky and danced to her timeless journey.

Jigonsahseh